T0368119

+ <u>BOOK TITLE:</u> "MULTIPLE WARHEAD ESSAYS" - BOOK I (UNEDITED EDITION)+

+ ABOUT EVOLUTION SCIENCE IN THE UNIVERSE, GOD, SATAN, AND THE FAULTY HOLY BIBLE. +

+ BY: REX CABAHUG, FROM WAIANAE, HAWAII, U.S.A.+

+ <u>GROUND ZERO:</u>

The whole Universe , which include all inhabitants and all existence in the entire Universe, without exception. And this book will serve as a catalyst to spark for the Universal Revolutions, in the entire Universe. Also to shed light about the beginning of everything in the entire Universe and the need to change mindset for all believers, at the obsolete Bible's wrong writings. And the need to stop being scammed and bullied into believing in hoaxes, at the obsolete Bible's book of Genesis, about God's creating Heaven and Earth and everything in the beginning of time in six days like magic, by just saying it. Such false claim from God which makes the Bible a fiction book, which is also considered a biggest super hoax of all time. Due to the poison effect that will contaminate the good content in that God's supposedly Holy book. Because due to the unbelievable writings at the book of Genesis, and other hoaxes at the obsolete Bible such as Armageddon, that is not real, and about Moses separating the ocean, for the Israelites to cross from Egypt, just like watching hoaxes-movies, which are not real. With these hoaxes, will make the Bible an unholy God's book, or become a fiction and imperfect, and impossible to imagine and believe, for a normal, educated and civilized creature in the Universe. Or are we still in the low I.Q., uneducated, uncivilized era, or like little children who don't understand and easily bullied, to just believe in anything that is not true. In which all the lawyers in the entire Universe would love to argue, for proof from God's creations of the Universe, for construction and evidence for super-mega factories that produces the stars, the planets, and all heavenly bodies in the Universe. And proof for God's super-mega creature workers, who handle the stars, planets, and all heavenly bodies in the entire Universe. Or such claim of creation in six days, is just God's wildest dream and imaginations, or without proof and

God cannot prove it. Therefore, such claim by God's creation is just a super hoax of all time and not true, as the lawyers to conclude for such mega claim by God, about his mega creations of the entire Universe, and everything in it, in just six days, as written in the book of Genesis in the Holy Bible, that is not true. Because the Universe happens to exist, through the Evolution Science process, and not by God's creation in six days. Since it took several countless trillion years of the Universe, non-stop of evolving and transforming, or nobody knows how long ago, in order to establish everything with the stars, planets, and all heavenly bodies, including everything that existed in the entire Universe, which did not happen too soon, as claimed by God in just six days of creation of the entire Universe ,which is false and should not be written at the Holy Bible, and wrong for all believers to continue believing in such a hoax. And based on those hoaxes at the obsolete Bible, wise Politicians and Lawmakers, are supposed to ban the use of the Bible for the solemn office oath taking, unless oath takers are drunk, or don't know some wrong contents in that obsolete unholy fiction Bible, which makes oath takers look like joking, and looks funny. Or you folks are serious or joking, swearing on a fictional and imperfect obsolete book of God. Based on the author's own belief.

+ This book is about Evolution Science, endless transformations for all existence in the entire Universe, as time goes on forever. All existence in the entire Universe is through Evolution Science is without exception, which include the existence of God, Satan, etc. or without Evolution Science, God, Satan, etc, doesn't exist at all including everything that existed in the entire Universe. Everything, which means all visible and invisible, good or bad, which includes countless trillions of evolving and transforming invisible germs and viruses, etc. Everything that existed in the entire Universe , through Evolution Science, 100% and no other means of existence in this Universe , where everything belongs and not by God's creation, as a lethal message to everyone in the entire Universe who happens to exist through Evolution Science only, or God is not behind it, as a fact, based on the author's own beliefs. +

+ 2023 Quote, based on the author's own belief: For all existence in the entire Universe . +

+ Once as part of the Universe, therefore will belong to the Universe forever, or each DNA will last forever. Similar to being born, then you become a part of the Universe, at the same time, you begin to belong to the Universe that will never end, and will last forever, or your forever journey of an endless evolving and transforming will continue without end. Such as a person dies, and will transform into an invisible spirit that will never die, but to continue the forever journey in evolving and transforming in the Universe. Whereas the dead body will decay to the ground, but it is not the end of it, because such decayed body is still part of the Universe that will never disappear. Since it will only transform into a different matter, as part of the Universe, in different forms of minerals, chemicals, and gas state, which will never disappear and will last, as part of the Universe forever, and it is still 100% total composition, or nothing is lost and still continue its journey of evolving and transforming forever in whatever form that will occur in the Universe. Where Evolution Science process that will last forever, is the only destiny for everything that existed, until eternity, once anyone happens to exist in the Universe . +

+ Once died, everyone will continue to embark their forever journey of evolving and transforming into a 100% invisible spirit, similar to a new birth, to the new invisible spirit world, based on everyone's DNA or blueprint, in which nothing is lost at all. Just like boiling a water which disappear from the pot, but transformed into a 100% invisible water vapor in which nothing is lost at all, and will continue to exist in the Universe forever. Similar to all other existence in the entire Universe that existed through Evolution Science, with all individual DNA's or all individual blueprints that will never disappear, or will last forever and will continue in evolving and transforming for each individual destinies towards infinity, moving up slowly and surely that will last forever 100% as time goes on. To become sophisticated and more powerful after evolving non-stop, as the only reward waiting for everyone that happens to exist in the Universe, that can not go wrong and unstoppable. No matter what happens in our destiny towards a forever journey of evolving, with our DNA's lifeline that will last forever, and will never disappear. +

+ In "MR. NO NAME's" world of Science, God is not recognized to exist, or there is no room for God's existence at all. In his formulas and equations and all his Scientific Discoveries, or all his life of Scientific adventures, especially in Physics, that mostly study about the existence of the entire Universe, which God doesn't exist in "NO NAME's" Science world. But this book welcomes God's existence with open arms and will explain that God existed through Evolution Science or without Evolution Science, God doesn't exist at all, as a fact based on the author's own beliefs, and to contradict "MR. NO NAME", for not recognizing about God's existence in the Universe, at his discoveries written in Science books. Or "NO NAME"consider that God and the Bible doesn't exist at all, or he only cares about his scientific discoveries, and not considering God as part of the Universe existence as a whole, which started its existence through Evolution Science. Starting from the birth of the Universe in the beginning of time, then after countless trillion years to pass the Universe grows and continued evolving and expanding. Starting to establish with the birth of the stars and all other heavenly bodies, evolving. Then God and company with all his angels started to evolve too, next to the Universe existence, and God and company become more powerful due to seniority, and considered as good evolvees who are motivated with positive attitudes. Then next to God's evolution is Satan and company with his demons, started to evolve behind from God in seniority and considered as bad evolvees, who are motivated with negative attitudes. Then all other evolvees followed with different seniorities, and everything that existed in the entire Universe through Evolution Science either good or bad and visible or invisible, in countless trillions, as part of the Universe that all existed and belong, starting to exist from Evolution Science with different seniorities. "MR. NO NAME" is not aware that his Scientific Theories are part of the Universe evolutionary existence processes and transformations as the Universe continues to evolve and transform forever. "NO NAME" is only after of discovering and wonder why it is happening, and not knowing the foundations behind it, in the beginning of time, when evolution begins and all those processes begins as well, and continue in evolving and transforming forever. Whereas formulas and equations will be derived, to find out what's going on, and why, or Scientists keep asking about the origin of the Universe in which they are not sure, or fully understand for explanations about Big Bang Theory, and about Black Hole, and etc. occurrences in the entire Universe. As it continues to evolve forever, in which they don't fully understand, or sure how it really started in the beginning of time. But based on the author's belief, it started from the total darkness and with a very tiny spark of energy, that gave birth to the Universe, and after several countless trillion years that has passed, or nobody knows for how long ago that has passed, the Universe has grown becoming super-mega Universe with everything existing with it, as it continues to evolve, and transform forever. +

+ This book is written based on the author's own thoughts and beliefs. And if any dispute about this book, you are advised to write your own book. Everyone is free to write their own book and express all your thoughts and beliefs, and please don't waste time arguing with the author. +

MULTIPLE WARHEAD ESSAYS

REX CABAHUG

Copyright © 2024 by Rex Cabahug.

Library of Congress Control Number:		2024905251
ISBN:	Softcover	979-8-3694-1792-8
	eBook	979-8-3694-1793-5

All rights reserved. No part of this book may be reproduced or transmitted in any form or by any means, electronic or mechanical, including photocopying, recording, or by any information storage and retrieval system, without permission in writing from the copyright owner.

Any people depicted in stock imagery provided by Getty Images are models, and such images are being used for illustrative purposes only.
Certain stock imagery © Getty Images.

Print information available on the last page.

Rev. date: 04/08/2024

To order additional copies of this book, contact:
Xlibris
844-714-8691
www.Xlibris.com
Orders@Xlibris.com
857682

ALOHA, OR HELLO!

WITH OUR FREEDOM OF THE PRESS, EVERYONE IS FREE
TO WRITE IN ORDER TO EXPRESS ALL YOUR THOUGHTS,
BASED ON YOUR BELIEFS … BUT I'M NOT PERFECT, OR
NOBODY IS PERFECT.

BY: REX CABAHUG,

72 YEARS OLD AUTHOR,

FROM WAIANAE, HAWAII, U.S.A.

+ In the beginning of time, it started in a complete total darkness similar to closing your eyes for a long time, then a very tiny flicker of almost invisible fainting light emerge, or a very tiny energy which started the birth of the Universe. Then after several countless trillion of years nobody knows how long of a very slow Evolving Science transformations processes and still continues now and forever as time goes on forever as well. It is that almost invisible tiniest flicker of energy, which become the driving force in the beginning of time that become the central source of energy for everything that ever existed throughout this wide and boundless Universe as we witness now after several countless trillion years that has passed and will continue forever, very slowly evolving and transforming with the infant Universe at the start, at trillion years old, still growing and starting to establish and expand with the birth of the stars, planets, and all heavenly bodies in the entire Universe, which all existed through Evolution Science, including the start of the existence of God, with his angels, known as good evolvees who are motivated with positive attitudes, and next to God in evolving is Satan with his demons who are considered bad evolvees who are motivated with negative attitudes. Both God and his angels and Satan with his demons are pioneers in evolution existence who have accumulated more powers due to their seniority in the evolution chart. Or the longer that they have evolved, they accumulate more power, existing in the Universe in countless trillion years, who are immortal, invisible, and etc. powers. Or God and company and Satan and company existed through Evolution Science about the same time the stars, planets, and all heavenly bodies started to establish with the Universe, during the growing period of the infant Universe in trillion years old. It means that it is the Universe who first existed, then followed by the existence of the stars, planets, and all heavenly bodies, together with the existence of God and company then Satan and company. Due to Evolution Science, everything existed which include the evolution of the Universe, the stars, planets, and all heavenly bodies, including God and company and Satan and company, and everything that existed in the entire Universe. Or without Evolution Science, nothing ever existed at all, including God doesn't exist at all. But everything will be credited to the first existence of the Universe at its birth, which have grown after countless trillion years that has passed, and continues to expand exponentially, or gaining more power and speed, as the Universe continues to evolve and transform forever. That very tiny flicker of energy that give birth to the Universe is expanding exponentially at present, is similar to a single stick of match to start a very small brush fire, and will expand exponentially, and compounding to become an unstoppable wildfire, that can burn the entire planet with steady source of fuel. So do the entire Universe will evolve and transform forever, more so with the vast and boundless sources of expanding energy as fuel to continue forever, to expand exponentially without end. Contrary to some scientist making some wild guess, or wild imaginations that the Universe existed and expanding due to the Big Bang theory, or black hole theory, which is not right because based on the author's own beliefs, that Big Bang and black hole, are just by-products as a result of the Universe original expansion exponentially and compounding, due to so much energy at present, bombarding everywhere with so much force exponentially and compounding to produce more power. And when we have so much mega force due to so much energy and compounding exponentially as the Universe expand, producing a compounded expansion exponentially, with the mini result of the Big Bang and black hole, as by-products from the Universe original product of compounded expansion exponentially process, as the Universe continues to expand forever, with boundless and endless source of energy. Starting from a very tiny almost invisible flicker of light, or energy in the beginning of time. And it is unstoppable, like a wildfire that will last forever, becoming a super-mega compounded exponentially energy that will sustain the entire Universe all existence forever, in our journey to an endless quest of evolving and transforming forever, as time goes on without end. Fueled by that almost invisible flicker of light, or the tiniest energy in the beginning of time that will last forever, as time goes on forever. Because of that tiniest energy, like a single stick of match to start, and becoming unstoppable wildfire, that will expand and compounding exponentially forever. As the Universe becoming a super-mega wide and boundless Universe, evolving and transforming non-stop, and everything in it which existed through Evolution Science, as time goes on forever. +

+ In Evolution Science, transformations, there are only two vertical directions to go, which is either positive transformations, or negative transformations, or up and down directions. Positive Evolution transformation, means an expanding growth in evolving process. While Negative Evolution transformation means the decaying or deterioration in evolving process. Or wherever it start to deteriorate from positive maximum growth, will start the negative transformation in evolving process. Or the Integral and Differential calculus of the Evolution Science transformation processes. For example, Mount Everest has reached its peak due to a positive growth moving upward due to a push from the Earth's crust or bottom, similar to volcanic push for lava upward, or its growth known as the positive transformation in Evolution Science. After reaching its maximum peak, or not moving up anymore, then negative or reverse transformations will take place, when it starts to deteriorate moving downward very slowly, or it depends to the conditions, as evolution science transformations process moves very slowly if not sooner, depending on the situation, until it reaches at the original sea level, after countless trillion years, or nobody knows how long it will take to occur. That's how Evolution Science works, with either positive or expanding, going up direction, or negative going down direction in evolving process, which means the decaying or deteriorating in evolving process. Similar to a person growing up, then after reaching its maximum growth, the negative process of evolving will take place, when you start to deteriorate and eventually decay after death, reaching the bottom line of your negative growth. Even diamonds, known to last forever, but it will still deteriorate or decay after it reaches its maximum limit of existence, then it will decay very slowly, invisible to the naked eyes, after countless trillion years, it will eventually deteriorate to a mere sparkling dust to its original existence, or whatever it is. As it will happen to anything depending on the evolution process that occurred, and with all sort of guessing and assuming such as recycling, and reincarnation, etc. But Evolution Science is the guiding blueprint for everything that existed in the entire Universe, and the author is not perfect for all kinds of analysis being introduce through this book. And about recycling, the author believes that everything will be recycled and depending to the process that occurred. For example an engine block can be recycled quickly by melting it at the furnace, but leaving it to rust, as a negative transformation process, that will take trillion of years or more, in order for that engine block to rust and decay to powder materials. That means everything can be recycled, if not sooner, but later after trillion years or more, and it depends to the situation or type of matters that existed in the Universe. Or even fuels like gasoline being burned to nothing, exiting at the exhaust chamber as carbon monoxide smoke, and will stay in the atmosphere, and eventually will come back as a raw oil, mined from the ground as recycled, and nobody knows for how long the process of an invisible evolving and transforming processes that will take place until it occurs. And other questionable recycling process for mankind such as reincarnation, that exactly the same person will be born again after death, assuming that a person becomes a sperm again, in order to be fertilized with a female egg, in order to be born again, or recycled like magic exactly the same, as an infant of course. With such assumption, the author will disagree, since it doesn't fit or coincide with the Evolution Science processes about recycling, or what kind of Biology Science process, this folks are thinking, or what kind of a dead person recycling technique and methods, that they use in order to obtain this kind of result for the reincarnation process, being born again the same. And such claim of reincarnation is totally different from cloning methods, in order to create duplicate human beings, and more duplicates if desired. And some scientist mentioned about the sun or stars dying or disappearing, but the author believe that those stars might just be transforming into another form of existence, as the process of evolving and transforming that will last forever

and will never disappear at all and will still stay, and still a part
of the Universe, no matter how it will deteriorate, or transform to
whatever result that the evolution process may produce, or recycling
processes, that will last forever in the Universe, in another form
of matter, or recycled, or like being born again into another form
of energy matter, or after countless trillion years to pass, being
recycled as a new form of energy in the Universe or whatever form,
since such energy emitted out and recycled back after countless
trillion years or more, will never disappear, and will continue the
endless journey of evolving, recycling, and transforming forever, to
whatever form of energy to exist in the Universe again, or a forever
cycle, and such energy will never disappear. With exception to the
Universe first or start of its existence, as a tiny flicker or spark
of energy, as the start of its birth from total darkness, that grow
and expand exponentially, with the birth of the stars, planets, and
all heavenly bodies and everything in it, to establish in the entire
Universe which all existed through Evolution Science process,
and will continue to expand exponentially forever. That means
the Universe will never die, like a dying star. That very energy at
the start, in the beginning of time, has expanded exponentially, as
we are witnessing at present, after several countless trillion years

that has passed, or nobody knows for how long the Universe has existed since its birth. Such very tiny energy in the beginning will never die or deteriorate, but become like a wildfire that will expand exponentially, and will last forever, unlike a dying star. +

+ NOTE FOR EXPONENTIAL COMPOUNDING EXPLANATIONS +

"X", to represent the Universe, with the exponent, on top of it shown below:

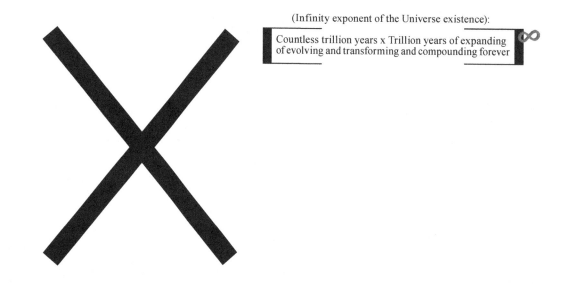

+ WAY TO GO OF NON-STOP IN EVOLVING AND TRANSFORMING FOR EVERYTHING IN THE ENTIRE UNIVERSE DUE TO THE ENDLESS AND UNSTOPPABLE SOURCE OF ENERGY IN THE UNIVERSE, THAT FUELS IT FOREVER, AND WILL CONTINUE TO EXPAND INFINITELY, OR WITHOUT END BECOMING MORE COMPLEX AS TIME

GOES ON FOREVER. AND FROM AN INFANT UNIVERSE IN THE BEGINNING OF TIME, WILL MATURE INTO A SUPER-MEGA UNIVERSE AS IT CONTINUES TO EXPAND EXPONENTIALLY, TRILLION YEARS UPON TRILLION MORE TIMES, TOWARDS A FOREVER ETERNITY, SINCE THE UNIVERSE WILL NEVER CEASE TO EXIST, OR WILL NEVER DISAPPEAR LIKE A DYING STAR. OR THIS ONE AND ONLY UNIVERSE WILL NEVER DIE, OR RECYCLED, AS AN EXCEPTION, AND MIGHT BE SIMILAR TO GOD'S OF FOREVER EXISTENCE, AND TO ALL WHO HAVE EVOLVED IN THE ENTIRE UNIVERSE, WHICH WILL TAKE COUNTLESS TRILLION YEARS TO ATTAIN, OF NON-STOP IN EVOLVING AND TRANSFORMING OR IT WON'T HAPPEN SOONER, TO GAIN THE POWER OF IMMORTALITY, AND A FOREVER EXISTENCE IN THE UNIVERSE. +

+ + + + +

+QUOTE OF ALL AGES, BASED ON THE AUTHOR'S OWN BELIEF+

+THE UNIVERSE IS INDEED THE SYNONYM TO BOUNDLESS WITHOUT LIMIT, ONE AND ONLY WITHOUT MATCH. THE MOTHER OF ALL EXISTENCE INCLUDING GOD, AND EVERYTHING WITHOUT EXCEPTION.+

+ We are witnessing how far mankind evolution and transformations has gone so far, gaining some little power, compared to God's super powerful status who has evolved so long in countless trillion years, or nobody knows how long ago. With continued progress, not in trillion years yet, mankind gain some little sophistications. Starting from the era, when mankind used to live in caves and the wilderness, naked like wild animals, homeless and used to run barefoot to travel. Now improve, with non-stop in evolving, from a naked caveman to a rocketman, used to run barefoot for travel, now with bullet train in order to travel faster, and can shoot up to the heavens above with space shuttles or space vehicles, and can live in space with space stations, and will eventually explore the heavens of the Universe, as we continue to evolve forever. And with all other improvements as we keep on evolving, with some little sophistications progress with all types of inventions in gadgets, computers, all types of vehicles, all types of machines, with homes, and high-rise buildings, and etc., since we use to dwell in caves, and wilderness, and homeless. That's the power of non-stop in evolving progress in this Universe in which we all belong. The longer we evolve, the more powerful we become, and we will ultimately attain Godly powers after countless trillion years in evolving, to become similar to God, and will become immortal, invisible, invincible, and can blend with all kinds of environments, such as God, transforming into a ball of fire as a holy spirit, based from the Bible, in order to live in the super-mega hot sun, or how can the sun torch God to nothing, when He become a ball of fire, or can transform into an invincible fish in order to live in the bottom of the ocean, or blend to any types of environment, or whatever it is. That's the power everyone can attain, and achieve, as the guaranteed waiting reward, after countless trillion years of non-stop in evolving and transforming, and will not happen sooner. As God has become super-powerful after evolving for countless trillion years that has passed, or nobody knows exactly, for how long ago since nobody is counting based on the author's own belief. And God will become super-mega God, as he continues to evolve forever to increase his power. And final important note with this essay, is to remind readers about God's existence based on the author's own belief. That God happens to exist in this Universe through Evolution Science process. Since God started to evolve in the Universe with human "DNA", through Evolution Science process only and no other means, or not that God appeared in the Universe like magic, for just coming out of nowhere instantly like magic. God should have a basis for his existence, that God started to evolve in the Universe through Evolution Science process, in order to exist. Or without the Universe, and without Evolution Science Process, God doesn't exist at all. And he doesn't exist through magic science, but he existed through Evolution Science and continue to evolve for countless trillion years to become super powerful, and he is considered to be the pioneer, or first to evolve in the Universe with a human "DNA" category to evolve, which is related or based, from his son "Jesus Christ," mentioned at the Bible, while dying at the cross and calling his invisible and super-powerful heavenly father, God. Sorry for some infos, as mentioned already at other essays at this book-just like hitting the bull's-eye target over and over again, or hitting "ground zero" over and over exactly at the same "GPS" target, and can not go wrong, based on the author's own beliefs. +

+ + + + +

+ Based on the author's own original belief, that the Universe is considered the Mother of all evolution existence in the entire Universe without exception including God who existed from evolution, or without evolution, God doesn't exist at all, and without the Mother Universe, nothing ever existed at all in the entire Universe, as a fact based on the author's own belief. And if the most powerful and invisible God has a human "DNA" related to his son, also the most famous "Jesus Christ," then there must be a science behind God's existence. But not magic science, for God to just come out from nowhere instantly, like magic and without basis, then started in the beginning of time, by creating the Universe and everything in it, in just six days, like magic. This is the reason why this book is written in order to explain, that it is "Evolution Science" process with God's human "DNA" when he started to evolve in the Universe, that is behind God's existence in the Universe. Also mentioned at other essays of this book, based on the author's own analysis and belief, that without evolution Science process, God doesn't exist at all, and without the Universe that provided for God's existence through Evolution Science process that occured inside the Universe, God doesn't exist at all. Not that God created the Universe, but instead it is the Universe who created God's existence in the Universe through Evolution Science process. And the bottom line, based on the explanations above, is similar to this events that occurred, as simple as this, that it is the Universe who give birth for God's existence in the Universe, as God started to evolve, in order to exist in the universe with a human "DNA" related to his son, Jesus Christ, or without the Universe, God can not exist at all. Therefore it is wrong, assuming that infant God claiming to have created his mother the Universe, or how can an infant God, do that to his mother the Universe, which is grossly wrong. As it is written at the Bible's book of Genesis, as proof about God's claim of creating the Universe and everything in it, in six days, like magic, which is considered by the author as the biggest hoax of all time, ever, and very impossible to imagine and believe, or it is just God's wildest dream, and imaginations of all time to claim of creating the Universe in six days. Because the Universe needs countless trillion years, of non-stop in evolving and transforming processes until now, in order to be established, with all the stars, the planets, and all heavenly bodies, and everything in the entire Universe. But not to be created by God in just six days, or not too soon just like a magic show. +

+ Based on the author's own belief, that God's human "DNA" variant during the time of God's start in evolving is a different human "DNA variant, with our present human "DNA" variant. Or both human "DNA" are the same, but with different variant category. Similar to Jesus Christ, possibly the same "DNA" variant with our present human "DNA" variant, but totally different human "DNA" variant with his heavenly father, who evolved several countless years ahead, compared with Jesus Christ human "DNA" variant. But the heavenly father is not alone, with his human "DNA" variant category during the time of his evolution or existence, which will include several countless angels of God, that has similar human "DNA" variants with God, during their era of evolving, or their start of existence in the Universe, which are considered as the pioneers in human "DNA" evolution, with different human "DNA" variant compared with our present human "DNA" variant, which is way behind compared to God's evolution seniority. That's why presently our human evolution progress is so behind and so much less powerful compared to God's super-powerful status, who has countless trillion years in evolving seniority from us, with the same human "DNA," but different human "DNA" variants, and a different era of evolving periods. That's why don't be confused why God is super-powerful, compared to us, who has the same human "DNA" with us, in which therefore suppose to be, we should be super-powerful similar to God. but as explained above that we have the same human "DNA" with God, but the different human "DNA" variants, is the one that makes the factual difference. And a very long period that separate us from God's era, or start of our evolving era, which is way behind from God, although with similar human "DNA" but different variants. And last note that Jesus Christ with similar human "DNA" variant with us, but known to have miraculous powers similar to God's power, but those powers are due to his invisible super-powerful heavenly father who is invisible but secretly assisting his only begotten son, which makes Jesus Christ obtain such powers. As Easter is celebrated, to show Jesus Christ power who died at the cross, then coming out alive from his grave, after being buried for three days, then ascended to heaven by elevating himself to the clouds above and disappear to the heavens above. Note that only Jesus Christ with similar DNA variant with our present human variant, that has super powers similar to his Heavenly Father God, due to Jesus Christ inherited it from his heavenly father's DNA variant. But none of us with present DNA variant similar to Jesus Christ that has power to come out from the grave and ascend to heaven above similar to Jesus Christ. Since we need countless trillion years to attain such power similar to Jesus Christ heavenly father, who has evolve countless trillion years in order to attain the power to come out from the grave and ascend to heaven. But with exception to Jesus Christ who inherited his heavenly father's very powerful DNA variant. Those are facts based on the author's own belief, and if any disagreements about the author's facts, you are advised to write your own book, and express all your beliefs and thoughts. Everyone is free to write their own book. +

+ Based on the author's own belief, that God's seniority in the evolution category originated together with the birth of the stars and other heavenly bodies, starting to evolve and grow to establish in the heavens after the birth of the Universe which started to expand, but still considered an infant Universe, after trillion of years that has passed, with non-stop of evolving and transforming, together with God's evolution, accumulating so much seniority in evolution rank, gaining more power, or considered most powerful based on his seniority or length of his evolving and transforming period becoming immortal, invisible, invincible and can blend with any types of environment, and etc. powers. Those are the facts that evolution and transformations moves very slow and surely, or not sooner, but after countless trillion of years to accumulate Godly powers, or based on seniority. Or the longer the evolution has occurred, the more power you accumulate, which happens to the very powerful God, who can transform into a ball of fire as a holy spirit mentioned at the Bible, therefore God can live in the surface of the super-mega hot sun as a ball of fire, in which the sun can not "torch" Him to nothing, since God transformed into a ball of fire, in order to blend with the sun's environment. And now we discuss about what happens to mankind evolution with much less seniority, maybe couple trillion years behind God's evolution period, or nobody knows how long is the difference of mankind evolution behind God's seniority. But with mankind continued evolving and transforming as we have witness at present we become a bit powerful with some little improvements in science, medicines, physics, biology, etc., and some little sophistications with inventions in machineries and all types of vehicles, and little advancement in technologies, with computers and different types of gadgets, etc. As mankind way back used to live in caves and the wilderness, homeless, and naked like wild animals, traveling while running with our barefoot. Compared at present as we gain some power after evolving and transforming a bit longer, now we have our bullet train, and etc. for traveling, with homes and high rise buildings to dwell. And from a naked caveman, has improved to a rocketman, as we continue to evolve, and can live and travel to the heavens of the universe, with our space stations and space shuttles, and etc. And as we improve in power with non-stop in evolving, while gaining more power as a guaranteed reward for everyone that existed in this Universe through Evolution Science as what happens to God's long seniority of continued evolving and transforming, now known to be most powerful, and God bragging based on his most powerful status, now claim to have created the Universe, in which the author, disputed this God's wrong claim for creating the Universe in six days like magic, at the Bible's book of Genesis in which the author disputed as a big hoax of all time, and not true. Or the Genesis writer might be crazy, or out of his mind who don't understand what he is writing. Since the truth, based on the author's own belief, that the Universe is the first that started to evolve as mentioned at other essays at this book, then after countless trillion of years of the Universe continued evolving and become established with the stars, planets, and other heavenly bodies, all starting to establish, then God started to evolve too, who is behind in seniority from the birth of the Universe evolution process for countless trillions of years, or for that long in order for the infant Universe with age at trillion years old, to establish with the stars, and other heavenly bodies evolving during those trillion years, as the infant Universe was growing and expanding. Therefore, God who is trillion years behind from the Universe existence, can not claim or brag that he created the Universe, instead it is the Universe who produces God's start in evolving, through Evolution Science process, in order for God to exist in this Universe. Or without the birth of the Universe, and without Evolution Science process in the Universe, God doesn't exist at all, and together with everything else, that existed in the entire Universe, as a fact, based on the author's own belief. And if anyone think that this book is a hoax, or disagree with the author, you are advised to write your own book, and don't waste time arguing with the author. Everyone is free to write their own book, and express all your thoughts and beliefs. +

+ Based on the author's own belief and analysis, about the secret behind the most famous God's existence in the entire Universe, will be analyzed similar to solving a puzzle for who's at no. 1 spot, or the top set of cubes, and who's at no. 2 spot, or the second set of cubes, and so on the third and fourth set of cubes, and etc. sequence based on seniority for all evolution existence in the entire Universe. In which we concentrate most on the first top spot, which belongs to the Universe first in existence, and the second set of cubes at no. 2 spot, which belong to God's existence, which is very controversial with conflicts and questions about God's existence and his creations, based at the book of Genesis at the Holy Bible, about God's magical creations of the entire Universe and everything in it in six days like magic, which is very impossible to believe, or all lawyers in the entire Universe would love to argue, for proof and truth. Or is this a super hoax written at the obsolete Holy Bible, which makes this book categorize as a fiction, with some other hoaxes stories about Armageddon, and stories about Moses separating the ocean, in order for the Israelites to cross at the bottom of the ocean floor, from Egypt to Israel, and etc. hoaxes. Those hoaxes of the Holy Bible, makes it unholy or imperfect, which might make believers change their mind, and will not believe the Holy Bible anymore. Or they are bullied and deceived to believe hoaxes for a long long time, about the false informations written at the obsolete Bible. Or are we still little kids who will just believe anything that is not true, or as adults, nobody complains. As the author explains at other essays at this book, that the Universe started to exist first. Which started in the beginning of time, from total darkness, then a tiniest flicker of an almost invisible light or energy emerge and the author considered it as the birth of the Universe, or the first existence of the Universe in order to claim the top spot for no. 1 cubes at the puzzle. Then for several countless trillion years, or nobody knows for how long the infant Universe has grown through Evolution Science process with non-stop of evolving and transforming while expanding and establish with the birth and the evolution of the stars, planets, and all heavenly bodies all existed too, and will be known as the Universe and company, as the first ones to evolve at no. 1, or the top spot at the puzzle cubes. Then God and company with his angels are the next to emerge and started to evolve through Evolution Science processes, at no. 2 spot at the puzzle cubes, and also considered as pioneers with the human DNA category of evolvee, based from Jesus Christ DNA, dying at the cross, calling his powerful and invisible heavenly Father God, in which therefore even without seeing God, it is assumed that God has a human DNA category. Since all existence in the entire Universe carry their individual different types of DNA categories. Now it is known that God's existence belongs at the no. 2 spot at the puzzle cube in sequence, or the next to evolve after the Universe, who is at the top or no. 1 cubes at the puzzle. Also note that the Universe and company has trillion years in seniority, or nobody knows how long, in order to establish in the Universe with the stars, planets, and all heavenly bodies before God and company emerge or started to evolve. Then subsequently, after countless trillion years of God's evolving and transforming which is considered having the most seniority, or pioneer in all evolvee with human DNA, God become very powerful as a result for evolving for a very long time in trillion years of non-stop evolving and transforming, as a guaranteed reward for long period of continued evolving, in which everyone gains more power. As based to our human evolution journey, not too long ago, not in trillion years yet, the author will just jump start our human evolution to the era when human started to live in caves and the wilderness naked like wild animals and homeless, has improved into a rocketman as we continue to evolve non-stop. Or from caveman to rocketman, is a huge leap already for mankind evolution power, and more progress in power is sure to come in our journey towards a forever existence through continued evolution in this Universe. While as of now, we notice already some progress or improvements and little sophistications as we gain little power or little rewards, as time goes on with our continued evolving and transforming that will last forever, and ultimately will attain Godly powers and more, after countless trillion years that will pass, of non-stop in evolving and transforming, but not sooner. As what happens to God who has evolve for countless trillion years becoming very powerful as his reward, who become immortal, invisible, invincible, and can blend with all types of environment, or can transform into a ball of fire, based from the Bible as a holy spirit, in which therefore, God can live in the surface of the super-mega hot sun. or how can the sun torch the ball of fire, in which God has transformed, due to his super power, or God can transform to blend with any kind of environment as mentioned at other essays at this book. Then based from God's very powerful status, and even if he is behind in countless trillion years from the Universe existence, God happens to be bragging with his very powerful status by acting like an outsider from the Universe, or coming out from nowhere, then claim that he created the Universe and everything in it in six days, like magic, as written at the book of Genesis at the Holy Bible, which is very impossible to believe as mentioned already. That's why the author doesn't agree, as being analyzed that how can God makes this claim as explained at the puzzle that God's rank at no. 2 in evolving rank from the birth of the Universe first existence in evolving. Since God existence in the Universe is trillion years behind from the Universe existence, then therefore, it is the Universe who provided the Evolution Science process, in order for God to exist, or without the Universe, and without Evolution Science, God doesn't exist at all, as a fact, based on the author's own analysis. Or God can not claim to create the Universe like magic, by just saying the words and done, acting like he is an outsider from the Universe making commands of creating the entire Universe in six days like magic, or like a dream which is not real, or a super big hoax of all time, that deceive and bullied the masses to believe it, for a very long time which makes that Bible so obsolete. Such wrong super claim by God's magical creation, is therefore corrected, that it is the Universe who provided God's existence through Evolution Science process, that happens inside the Universe as said, that without the Universe, and without the Evolution Science that provided for God's start in evolving, and transforming that occurred inside the Universe, then God doesn't exist at all. But not that God acting like an outsider from the Universe, coming out from nowhere to command that the Universe be created like magic, but instead it is the Universe that created, or provided for God's existence in the Universe through Evolution Science process. As said that the Universe existed first through Evolution Science process, but not that God created the Universe, or such claim by God is a super hoax, or such claim by God is without basis, since God existed in the Universe through Evolution Science, behind from the existence of the Universe which is the first to exist through Evolution Science, then God existence followed, who is trillion years behind from the Universe existence. This is the controversial conflict here in this Universe in order to obtain the truth about this puzzle, which is the existence of the Universe through Evolution Science process, versus God's claim of creating the Universe in six days like magic, or how can it happen, and might be a hoax or not true, but such claim by God will still stand, as it is written at the Holy Bible and embrace by all believers. But based on this book about Evolution Science, the author will express his own belief, consider this facts that both the Universe and God existed through

Evolution Science, or without Evolution Science, the Universe and God doesn't exist at all, and that it is the Universe who is the first to evolve, then God's existence through Evolution Science in the Universe is next to the Universe existence. Therefore, God cannot claim to create the Universe, because God can not exist in the Universe without the Universe first existence. That's how to settle this disputed conflict at the puzzle, that the Universe is first to exist or first to evolve, or no. 1 at the top of the puzzle cube, then followed by God's existence, or next to the Universe to evolve, or no. 2 at the puzzle cube. Or God cannot be on top at no. 1 spot cubes, in order to create the Universe in six days like magic. Because everything that existed in the entire Universe occurred through Evolution Science only and no other means, which is happening very slowly, in countless trillion years, but not too soon, similar to God's magical creations in six days, in creating the Universe and everything in it, which is a super hoax of all time, which makes the obsolete Bible a fiction book, unholy, and imperfect God's Holy book, due to the poison effect that will contaminate the good contents in that book, and to put the blame on those few entry of some false informations, at the Bible's book of Genesis, about God's creation of the Universe and everything in it, in just six days without proof, and other hoaxes about Armageddon, and story about Moses separating the deep ocean, for the Israelites to cross at the seafloor fleeing from Egypt, and etc. hoaxes, just like watching movies that are not true. Because the true existence of the Universe since its birth, took several countless trillion years until now, in order to establish with the stars, the planets, and all heavenly bodies in the Universe, including everything that existed in the entire Universe through Evolution Science processes only and not by God's creation in just six days, as written in Genesis at the Holy Bible, which is considered as God's magical creation, or it is just God's wildest dream, and imaginations which is not real. Since it took several countless trillion years, in order for the entire Universe to evolve and exist through Evolution Science process, and not by God creating the entire Universe in just six days like magic. Or God might be touching-down in Las Vegas, for a super-famous magic show of all time. By the super-famous magician in the Universe, God our fellow co-evolvee, who claimed to have created the entire Universe in six days, by just saying it like a magic show, as written at the Holy Bible's, Book of Genesis. +

+   +   +   +   +

+ As we move into the next stage in our evolution journey of transforming into the invisible spirit world after death, is similar to being born again into a new different spirit world, in which a new life begins in the new invisible spirit world. Then the law of Evolution Science applies, in which the spirit world can not go back to the previous world behind, or the new elevated invisible spirit world can not mix-up with the physical living world in this planet Earth, and other planets in the entire Universe, and can not do any business matters whatsoever. Just like expecting something to be accomplished by praying, or calling the spirits of the dead to help you win the lottery, or any other stuff in which the spirit world can not help at all to let you win, or accomplished whatever you wish. Or any occurrences of happening, after praying or chanting to the invisible spirit world is just a matter of coincidence or apparently by mere chance or pure luck, but not as a result of praying or chanting to spirits, which is just a waste of time or useless, because in the Evolution Science process, prayers or chanting doesn't help at all. Things happen to evolve and transform naturally non-stop, after countless of years to pass, as time goes on forever without help from prayers or chanting, and etc., rites and rituals.+

+ This book will also shed light about the origin of everything that existed through Evolution Science in the entire Universe visible and invisible. Imagine if you pick up a tiny single grain of sand at the beach, and that tiny sand represent our planet Earth in the entire boundless Universe in which everything belongs, out of countless several trillion of sands at the beach, which represents the stars, the planets, etc. and everything in this boundless Universe. Imagine how tiny and invisible our planet Earth, similar to a tiny grain of sand, where we all belong, existing as part of the Universe and due to Evolution Science, we will continue to exist, and transforming as we evolve forever together with the Universe and everything in it, as time goes on forever. And those stars, planets, and everything in the entire Universe mentioned above, are the product of several countless trillion of years by non-stop of evolving and transforming, and not as a result by God's magical creations in six days, at the Bible's book of Genesis. And this is a fact, based on the author's own beliefs. If anyone to disagree, is advised to write your own book and express all your opinion and beliefs, instead of wasting time arguing with the author, for whatever reasons related to this book. +

+ Note about this simple and significant example about Evolution Science Natural Process. That the beaches at the ocean shores doesn't appear like magic, similar to God's claim of his magical creation of the Universe, which is false. As we know that beaches at the shores, appear either white sand beach, or black sand beaches especially in Hawaii. Or it depends to the type of coral rocks that are being pounded and grinded by the ocean waves for countless trillion years, then appears at these beaches at the ocean shores, which did not happen like magic, but through natural Evolutioin Science process, or not as a result of God's magical creation, like beaches appeared instantly like magic. But it started with the raw materials of a white coral rocks, or black coral rocks being pounded and grinded by the ocean waves, for countless trillion years, or not too soon. Then as the grinded coral sand being pushed by the ocean waves to the shores, which created either white or black sand beaches, as seen as the finished product appearing at the ocean shores and beaches, which did not occur too soon as mentioned, or not by God's magical creation in order for these beaches to appear, either white or black sand beaches. Which all depends to the type of coral rocks being pounded and grinded by the ocean waves without magic being involved, but through a very long period of time that has passed, based on the Evolution Science natural process. And therefore, no longer wonder why, we have these white or black sand beaches, etc., in which nobody created it like magic. And imagine how long it took for all those sands to accumulate at the beaches, as an example of the negative deterioration of those dead coral rocks going through the differential calculus, or the negative Evolution Science process, by turning into grain of sands, with the ocean waves constant pounding and grinding non-stop, as the coral rocks evolve into grain of sands at the beaches. +

+ Based on reality check: It is real that God is written at the Bible's book of Genesis, well-known for his supernatural powers, and bragging to create the Universe and everything in it in just six days, in which believers agree and embrace the Bible without complaining, and believe in God in their heart. As God to all his believers and religious followers, then why can't God help, using his supernatural powers in order to help and stop all kinds of calamities that we are experiencing here on planet Earth. Since God acknowledge his presence in the Bible, then why can't he act accordingly to show his supernatural powers in order to stop the sufferings of the masses, as he is powerful to know everything that is happening everywhere in the entire Universe that he created, and to be known that he is God to all and creator of everything, listening to everything, and seeing everything based on his supernatural powers. As it is known in the Bible, or it is just hoaxes of all ages at the Bible that deceive and bullied believers to believe on falsehood at the obsolete Bible, similar to reading a fiction book that is not true. Although there are some good stories in that book, but being contaminated with falsehood and imperfect, if God's power is not for real, or considered hoaxes stories of God's powers, just like believers are watching movies that is not true. And believers sufferings with all calamities, are for real that needs help and supposed to, God can help very easily with his supernatural powers, but no help. Pretty much easier than creating the entire Universe in six days, and if he is truly the powerful God of the entire Universe, as it is written at the Holy Bible for real, and for everyone to believe it, or not. As based at the Bible about God's most powerful status that he created the Universe, then stopping the calamities is easier for God to do, or stopping wars by sending legions of God's angels as peacekeepers, to disable weapons between conflicting armies, or everything is possible for God who is well-known for his super-powers at the Bible. Or God to harness his supernatural power by stopping catastrophic wildfires, etc. by dumping heavy rain, which is very easy for God to do, compared to creating the Universe in six days, if his supernatural power is real, or a hoax. And as His powerful begotten son, Jesus Christ is known to stop a storm through his command, as written at the Bible's New Testament tales, and even known to have power to walk above the ocean, without sinking and etc. supernatural powers, that he show-up similar to his Heavenly Father. Or why not the Heavenly Father and Jesus Christ his son, work together to help believers and worshippers like a family in God, as they are praying to God and Jesus Christ everyday, as Holy masses and prayers are performed by church workers and believers everyday. Or else both the Heavenly Father and Jesus Christ supernatural powers are just useless if not used at all, in helping the family of God in the Universe, which is very easy for both to do, without turning their back, or they doesn't care at all, for all cries and sufferings of victims of calamaties, asking for God and Jesus Christ for help, but no help from both at all. Or nobody is listening at all, just like talking to a statue who cannot help at all. Or is there anything else that can not be done by God, and for what reason that it can not be done by God, or is there anybody else who is more powerful than God, that God is afraid to do so, for some sort of penalty for acting like a loose cannon, as long as it is not an evil motivation, as he is God of righteousness. Or God needs to follow rules at all, and who's imposing the rules from where? Or God is afraid to be punished and to perish into oblivion, like he never existed at all in the Universe. And who will impose such punishment, or is there anybody else who is more powerful than God, to impose such punishment to God? Or what is God's reason for not helping those believers who are suffering, or stop the calamities, and wars sooner than later, if he is truly the God in the Universe, for all believers who ask God for help at their prayers, but no effect. When in fact, based from the Bible about God's supernatural powers, that it is possible for God to act like a loose cannon to use his powers for righteousness sake, in order to help stop all calamities and wars, for all God's children, or God's family in the Universe, from all kinds of sufferings. And that's how the heavenly father is suppose to act immediately, in order to protect his family, similar to all other family, to act like a loose cannon in harnessing his super-powers, to protect his family, during the need for urgent help such as stopping a war, or re-directing a hurricane towards the sky as soon as possible, and etc. calamities and sufferings. But God is afraid to do so, as it is happening all the time. Or whom that God is afraid of, in order to harness his immediate help for righteousness sake. Is God afraid of Satan who will stop him, and might dethrone him as ruler of the Universe. And if God is dethroned by Satan, then what will happen next, is God afraid that the Universe and everything will perish to oblivion, which will include God and Satan, will perish to oblivion too. But based on the author's own belief that the Universe will not perish to oblivion, and God is not suppose to hesitate in acting like a loose cannon, in harnessing his superpowers to stop anything bad that is happening to his family in the Universe, for righteousness sake, and not afraid of Satan for stopping his moves for whatever reason, and for righteousness sake. But now everybody in the Universe is assuming that God is afraid of Satan who will stop him for acting like a loose cannon in harnessing his superpower, and might dethrone God as ruler of the Universe. Just like everybody in the Universe is watching a forever movie, about this two super-famous actors endless competition, between God and Satan in the Universe. And that God might be afraid that he will perish to oblivion, if Satan dethrone him, and might be scared that his super-powers will diminish, if he uses such powers like a loose cannon, in order to render urgent and immediate help to his children and creations in the Universe, as a family in God. Or what kind of heavenly father he is to neglect his family, because Satan might stop him, and that's one of the valid reason why he is afraid of doing so. In which suppose to, he will not be afraid of Satan to stop him, in order to do whatever he wants for righteousness sake, as he is known in the Bible as God of righteousness. But due to God's in-action in rendering immediate help, like stopping wars, and hurricanes, and etc. calamities, and sufferings, using his super-powers which is not happening, and Satan might be stopping God, or God is afraid of Satan stopping him are the other two reasons behind it. But God is not suppose to be afraid of Satan, when he can stop Satan too. Then why God is scared about Satan stopping him for whatever that he wants to do for righteousness sake, especially during urgent need for help sooner to his family in the Universe. Or Satan will get his negative evil ways due to God's in-action, and what will happen next if God will allow Satan to rule the Universe. Or are we watching similar to a never ending movie about God and Satan endless competition, and who will prevail and win this competition. Or all of these assumptions by the author are just fictions, based on his own thoughts and beliefs. But the August 8, 2023, Maui catastrophic fires especially in Lahaina, and other catastrophic calamities, including victims and sufferings due to wars, and all other catastrophic sufferings in this planet are not fictions. In which God and Jesus Christ supernatural powers are just useless as said, if not use at all, during urgent need for help. As believers keep calling God and Jesus Christ for help, Oh my God, my Heavenly Father and Jesus Christ, where are you hiding? Please show us your supernatural powers, for stopping this catastrophic fires in Maui, by dumping that heavy rain in order to stop these fires instantly, which is very easy for both to do as a miracle. Or both doesn't care at all, even how much you have prayed and offerings being performed, just like talking to a statue who can not help at all, as mentioned already. But Jesus Christ is suppose to help too, as soon as possible to help his Heavenly Father. As Jesus Christ using his supernatural powers, is known to stop a storm, by talking to the wind, in order to stop causing havoc and destruction, or Jesus Christ has the supernatural powers to control the forces of nature, that his Heavenly Father created. As it is written at the Bible, or is this just another hoax story from the son of God. Or if Jesus Christ supernatural powers are real or not, for stopping catastrophic calamities sooner, and if not used are just useless if it is not a hoax, or Jesus Christ might be hiding, together with his Heavenly Father.

Therefore it doesn't make sense calling them for help. Or Jesus Christ is still hiding and afraid to come out, might be thinking that he is still "WANTED" dead or alive by the Roman soldiers, who might arrest him, and crucify him again. That's one of the reason for no show for him, for a very long time. And all his believers are hungry and waiting for his return and miracles to occur. Especially during sufferings due to catastrophic calamities and tragedies, for his entire family in God, in this planet who needs his immediate help ASAP, and as our VIP and guaranteed savior, who is the only begotten son of our Heavenly Father God. That's why everybody is waiting and excited for his triumphant return to this planet Earth, but when will it is going to happen, nobody knows. But he made a promise that he will come back like a thief, as said in the Holy Bible. Maybe to avoid being detected by the Roman soldiers, who might arrest him by surprise as a "WANTED" person, and might crucify him again. Or Jesus Christ needs some counseling to change his mind-set, not to be afraid of the Roman soldiers anymore, since the Roman Empire has already collapsed for a very long time, and no longer exist, and nobody is going to arrest and crucify him again. So, no need hide, and time to come out from your hiding place, in order to perform those miracles that all believers are waiting for a very long time already. And don't act like a thief anymore, to avoid getting detected by the Roman soldiers. That's why he needs to reset his memory about the past, that the Roman soldiers no longer pursue after him like a "WANTED" man to be captured again, as what happens long time ago, and not to be crucified at the cross again. So that he can come out from his hiding place, and help those who are suffering on Earth. And not wasting his miraculous supernatural powers similar to his Heavenly Father God. Based on the author's own assumptions, and beliefs if it is true, as revealed at the Holy Bible. And if both are truly hiding by not helping at all, in spite of their supernatural powers which is just useless, and why they are not using it, for righteousness sake.

+   +   +   +   +

+ LAST QUOTE FROM THE AUTHOR: +

This book is my unpolished diamond on the rough. And will serve as a legacy of my life for becoming an author, in which I never expected to happen in my lifetime. Based on my wildest dreams and imaginations, coupled with my own thoughts and beliefs, this book is created and will last forever, together with the Universe to exist forever. And no matter what will happen to this book, or being recycled to a different form of matter, its legacy or blueprint, will never disappear, in this one and only Mother Universe of all existence, in which everything belongs forever until eternity, and everything to continue the forever journey of evolving and transforming. Based on Evolution Science natural process, and no other means in this Universe for all existence.

+ + + + +

+ JUST FOR HUMOR, FROM THE AUTHOR: +

A lot of Inventors becoming billionaires, by selling their products like hot cakes. Now watch out for this Hawaiian Cowboy from Waianae, a 72 years old Senior Citizen, will be selling at least a billion books in one year, with book buyers around the world. And will become an instant billionaire in one year time, if everyone in this planet will own this book easily without bragging. But sorry, for such an ambitious goal is just a hoax, and I am not a real cowboy. Just an ordinary citizen living in Waianae, Hawaii. Keep thriving, never give up, and always be humble. Since there is no limit for anyone to be successful in this boundless Universe, where everything belongs forever. Good luck, and best regards to everyone. ALOHA OR GOOD-BY, and my next book is coming soon. +

+ ALOHA, FROM REX CABAHUG, OF WAIANAE, HAWAII, U.S.A. +

+ AND MAHALO, OR THANK YOU TO ALL. +

+ WITH SPECIAL THANKS:+

To my first granddaughter, Jadenne Radoc Cabahug, a 2023 Journalism Graduate, at the University of Washington in Seattle, for helping type my manuscript in order to help me publish this book.

+ + + + +

+ ALOHA +

Printed in the United States
by Baker & Taylor Publisher Services